To Robbi

    Hapr
sure fu
Pennsylvania ~~~~~~
Williamsport. Hope you enjoy
these funny stories.

      Love,
        Gramma

May 2021

The Headless Dog

&

Other Extraordinary

Far Fetched

True Tales

Of Central Pennsylvania

Written by

Beverley Conrad and Gregory Burgess

Illustrated by Beverley Conrad

Except where otherwise noted

Cover Photo by Joslyn McKenzie

Second Printing 2014

Printed in the United States of America

ISBN: 13:978-0-9899382-0-4
Requests for permission to make copies of any part of the work should be mailed to:
Beverley Conrad and Gregory Burgess,
42 Music Row Lane, Selinsgrove, PA 17870
bevconrad@yahoo.com

Additional copies of The Headless Dog and Other Extraordinary Far Fetched True Tales of Central Pennsylvania

Published by:
Salem Swamp Press
42 Music Row Lane
Selinsgrove, PA 17870
USA
570-374-2647

www.salemswamp.com

Contents

Introduction..1

Dog Heaven 4

Beachy's Place 9

Big Brown George Row...................................15

The Pow-Wower 20

Ghosts of Governor Snyder Mansion 27

Mother's Helper..35

Penn's Tavern 39

The Phantom Fiddler of Paddy Mountain..............48

The Headless Dog..56

The White Woman of Montgomery's Bar..............63

Trailer - Free! Will Deliver! 68

The Painter 73

Big Brown Panther..76

Owl Medicine...78

Acknowledgments

We would like to thank those people who shared their stories with us for the creation of this book, and the sleepless nights, I might add. Bob Musser told us the one about the dog and **Dog Heaven.** He shared a great many stories about experiences at Penn's Tavern, some of which are included in the story of **Penn's Tavern.**

The experiences of sightings in **The Beachy Place** were told to me by a woman who lived there for a while with her four children. We used to wait together for all of our kids to get off the school bus and she would talk. You have to love people who will talk!

We thank the artist, the late John R. Johnson, for the pen and ink sketches he did of us performing at **Penn's Tavern** as well as the sketch of the tavern itself. A curious story goes along with that sketch. It was scanned from the original copy that hung in the tavern for many years and one night when a few people who sat around the bar were discussing "the ghosts" the picture just jumped off the wall and fell to the floor! The frame broke, but the glass didn't. Thank you, John, wherever you are…

The story of **Big Brown George Row** happened here in the house where we now live in Salem Swamp. Greg has drawn from our daughter, Joslyn McKenzie's, experiences when she was a child. Joslyn also provided the cover photo for this book. She's particularly adept at creating spooky effects, maybe from having grown up in a haunted house. We should probably toss in a thank you to her brother and our son, James Burgess, for blowing the head off what was a nice statue of a dog until the day he used it for target practice with his paintball gun. We didn't thank him at the time but it came in handy for the cover photo on this book.

The story of **The Pow-Wower** happened to Greg and is a true story of his experience of visiting the pow-wower.

We would like to thank Diane Mann and Scott (last name withheld) for sharing their stories of **Ghosts of the Governor Snyder Mansion.**

Georgie Hoagland told me the story about **Mother's Helper.** You've got to love chatting with a woman behind a shop counter on a slow day, especially one who has such good stories to tell!

Somebody told me there was a fiddler who was supposed to haunt the top of Paddy Mountain, but I honestly can't remember who told me. Be that as it may, I made up most of the story of **The Phantom Fiddler of Paddy Mountain**, but you never know. Maybe this is the way it really happened.

The Headless Dog is a collection of tales of the Bloody Triangle, the area that surrounds our house. Greg found these stories through his research of local history and legends about Snyder County and he wove those into a tale.

The White Woman of Montgomery's Bar is another story that I heard somewhere, but can't remember the source, I've known it for so long. I didn't conjure this one up, though. Supposedly, there is a ghost that haunts that part of the riverbank, and supposedly, this is how she got there.

Trailer - Free! Will Deliver! was told me late one night around a campfire in the woods by C.A.Y. (name withheld at the request of the storyteller.) We were at a jam session and as the music died down as well as the campfire she told me this story, this true story, of what happened to her on that very spot. Scared the wits out of me, it did. Thank you.

The Painter happened to me. I'll tell this story any time the conversation turns to the subject of the eastern cougar, a panther, or of odd sightings while in the woods. Greg wrote a song about this sighting and we'd like to thank Sandy Bruce for the fine painting she did for Greg about this jazzy, big brown panther.

When you read your way through this book, in the story **Owl Medicine** you will find repetitive threads. Certain characters mentioned in previous stories resurface under different names, and certain places and areas will seem familiar to you. Sometimes the stories just weave themselves together into a new piece of fabric and that is what happened with this one.

The following stories were previously published:

"The Headless Dog" by Gregory Burgess appeared as "The Headless Dog and The Bloody Triangle" in *Paranormal Pennsylvania and Beyond*, July 2003 Issue 5.

"Penn's Tavern" by Beverley Conrad appeared in *Paranormal Pennsylvania and Beyond*, October 2003 Issue 6.

"Ghosts of the Governor Snyder Mansion" by Gregory Burgess appeared in *Paranormal Pennsylvania and Beyond*, January 2004 Issue 7.

"The Phantom Fiddler of Paddy Mountain" appeared in *Fiddler Magazine*, Fall 2002 Volume 9 Number 3.

Introduction

I believe in ghosts. I once saw one. But it didn't happen here in the Susquehanna River Valley, so that story is not included in this book. Our daughter saw a ghost. In fact, she has seen several ghosts. She saw them in the house we now live in - The Row House in Salem Swamp. That story is included in this book. I didn't see those ghosts because I didn't want to see them. In fact, as a rule, I never want to see them. I don't quite understand what a ghost is, you see.

Is a ghost really a person come back from the dead? Or is a ghost more like an escaped image from a television screen? Is a ghost a memory made flesh (or rather spirit) by our imaginations? Is it created from a desire to have them here with us so that we can see them? I don't know.

The stories in this book were for the most part collected from the stories other people have told us about their sightings and experiences. These stories were told late at night during conversations after hours at the place where we work, Penn's Tavern, which is severely haunted, I might add. They were told to us sometimes in broad daylight over store counters, in parks, at get-togethers. All we'd have to do sometimes was mention that we worked at Penn's Tavern and the first question would be, "Hey! Is that place as haunted as they say it is?" And one story would lead to another and pretty soon they would tell their story. And of those, there are some pretty good ones floating around the valley. Those stories are included in this book.

Some of the stories in this book have been researched and include a fair amount of local history. Some of the stories are just laid out as they were told to us. As the saying goes, "I don't know if this story is true, but as it was told to me, I'll tell it to you." Some of the stories have been fictionalized in a sense as a way of not using real names. The final story in this book is a collection of weird events and occurrences - all true. As I was writing it down one night it began to take form and I found that the remembrance of one occurrence led to the memory of another. As I recall, at the time, that seemed to be exactly what happened in real life.

Now about that ghost that I saw - once! And I stress, only once! It happened a long time ago, many miles from here, and I was working in a house where other workers said they had seen a ghost and that they had heard the place was haunted and one day – in broad daylight - I looked down a hallway and saw a woman walk from one room to the next - not really walk - more like she glided - and I kept my eyes right on the doorway to the room she entered which had only one entrance - and walked into the room and it was empty! So I'd say I saw a ghost! But that's another story…

~Beverley

Dog Heaven

Does a dog have a soul? Does this beast of the earth that has accompanied man since the days of prehistory have an essence, a spirit that can outlast the bonds of physical being? Do dogs go to Heaven?

Times when people have lived through the death of a well-loved pet, they have often consoled themselves with the comforting thought that one day they would meet their dog again, one day beyond the shadow of Mother Earth, one day in Heaven.   Imagination persists when one thinks of a dog heaven. What is Heaven to a dog?

Is it a dinner table set for Thanksgiving and all the people are out and the table is only a foot high? Is it being able to lie at its master's feet and have its ears, belly and back scratched for all eternity? Is it a wild run without a leash, through fields of green filled with the scent of woodchucks, squirrels and rabbits that offer endless chase?

Perhaps it is where dogs go when they dream. Many people have witnessed a sleeping dog dreaming away during one of its many naps - the nose twitches, the lips tense slightly as if to bark. One might hear whimpers and muffled whines as the dog tries to run, its paws jerking through - what? Invisible fields of high grass, luscious scents, and damp woodlands. "He's after a rabbit," some will say as they reach down to scratch behind the ears of their loyal companion. "Yeah, old boy - that's good. You get that rabbit now." The dog might drowsily open one eye, pulled back to the waking world by its master's voice as the "rabbit" takes off through the fields of green - through Dog Heaven.

One summer day in 1988 Bob and his nephew Rag, decided to head down to Hallowing Run. Hallowing Run is a creek that winds its way through the valley between Augustaville and Fisher's Ferry on the east side of the Susquehanna River. A road follows the creek and is appropriately named Hallowing Run Road. Bob and his nephew felt like hunting that day. Maybe they'd get lucky and bring home some small game for supper. Shouldering their shotguns, they headed up Hallowing Run Road, then decided to cut across a field of fresh mowed alfalfa. The hunting might be better in the weeds between the field and

5

the nearby woods. They were about a quarter mile from the road when company showed up - company in the shape of a dog.

Might it disturb their own hunting? Didn't seem like it. This dog was on a trail of its own. Tail high and curled over its back, the gray, Husky-type dog must have found some hot scent from the way it shuffled and sniffed through the high grass and weeds that bordered the field. Bob said he could see the tall grass separate as the dog cut its way through the weeds. Bob figures it wasn't any more than twenty to thirty feet away from them but it paid them no heed. A dog in pursuit of a rabbit or woodchuck is a dog in its own world.

Bob and Rag stayed with the dog for a short spell, keeping a polite distance mind you, but close enough to see every hair on its back as it rose occasionally from the grass to sniff the air more precisely. The cicadas hummed their hot summer day song; the bees buzzed; the occasional call of a bird sounded. Yet for all they could see the dog, and if either one had stepped forward fast enough, perhaps they could have touched the dog, they could not hear their companion's movement.

They stopped to watch the dog for a bit, let him move ahead a little ways. They had after all almost caught up to him. Only ten feet separated the two hunting parties. The dog stood still, cast the air for the scent again, tail high, head erect, ears peaked forward-- then it disappeared.

Bob stood still for a minute or so staring at the place

the dog had been before saying anything to Rag. Rag didn't talk right away either. Bob spoke first.

"What did you just see, Rag?"

"A dog."

"Color?"

"Grey."

"Hunting?"

"After something."

"Then what?"

"Nothing. I don't know what happened to it. It just - faded."

"Let's get outta here."

Ghost dog? Ghost stories often have to do with earthbound spirits that have somehow been left behind due to a sudden tragic end or perhaps the longing to complete unfinished business. The spirit conveys that feeling of sadness or frustration to the viewer who chances to glimpse it. But this dog was in high spirits. His tail held high over his back, he bounded, ruffled, sniffed and tramped his way through the warm, scent-filled grass, bowing occasionally to nuzzle the damp, warm earth. He was a dog in command, on the trail of something, and to Bob and Rag he was a pure joy to witness.

What was it that Bob and Rag witnessed that summer day near the field on the way to Hallowing Run? Did they catch sight of a ghost, a dog somehow still tethered to the world where they lived? Maybe, just maybe they were favored with a momentary freedom, a lucky step that allowed them a brief glimpse beyond their world - and into Dog Heaven.

Beachy's Place

Portrait of Martin Beachy by Beverley Conrad

In the broad valley just over the ridge from the tiny village of Salem, the fingertip fogs cling to the swampy wetlands that border the creek - the lowest point of the valley. On warm spring evenings the sounds of tree peepers fill the damp air with their plaintive mating calls.

Near the creek on Salem Road there was a farmhouse, old barn and a few outbuildings - all in need of repair. The farm was known to locals as "Beachy's place." The house, when this story was written, was vacant - vacant since the murder of Martin Beachy.

Martin Beachy was one of Snyder County's most colorful characters. A true businessman by nature, he abandoned the farming profession to take up that of buying and selling antiques and used goods. Some people called it junk, but gold takes on different forms to each person. Some find treasure in trash.

Martin Beachy built the 522 Auction Barn on Route 522 in Penn Township and made it successful as a flea market and auction house. Every Friday night people would stream in from miles around in cars, trucks, and horse and buggy. They would socialize and eat, buy and bid. For ten years since the auction barn first opened in 1982, people did this - until that Saturday night in May, 1992 when Martin Beachy was murdered. The newspapers said he was murdered for money. Because of the ritualistic style to the murder, however, rumors flew among the locals that Beachy was the victim of witchcraft.

Martin Beachy married his first wife, Mary, and lived in the white farmhouse with her for many years, raising a family of ten children. Mary died in the early eighties following a long illness. Those who knew Beachy say that he was inconsolable. He was purely and truly grief stricken. In fact, in order to preserve the memory of Mary Beachy, it was said that he locked the door of the room where she died, thereby keeping everything in tact as it had been the day of her death. Pill bottles still stood on the nightstand. Sheets, once slept on by the dying woman, still covered the bed.

Portrait of Mary Beachy by Beverley Conrad

A few years later Martin Beachy enjoyed a brief marriage to a woman fifty years his junior. The woman refused to move into the white farmhouse. She told Beachy that Mary was still there, that she had seen her. And that Mary did not want her in the house. Beachy complied and moved into a second house he owned in the valley - the one up on the hill.

Shortly before his death, Beachy rented the white farmhouse by the creek to a family of six. The children ranged in age from ten to about sixteen. Beachy gave strict orders to the tenants not to open the locked bedroom door. The room was off limits. The family claimed that the white house on Salem Road was haunted - haunted by the spirit of Martin Beachy's first wife, Mary.

Though a family with four active children should have brought cheer to the house, on entering it one felt a gloom, a pervasive feeling of frustration and sadness. The house even on sunny days appeared dark inside. The children were afraid to go upstairs alone. And in that house, especially upstairs, they never turned off all the lights. The children had heard someone walking about in the dark when no one should have been. The little girl would coax her old dog, Jack, to accompany her on trips to the upstairs bathroom. She would tug at his collar, pulling the reluctant mutt up the stairs with her just so she would not have to be alone, just in case the footsteps of the invisible inhabitant sounded through the hallway.

One night a cousin slept over. As usual, the hallway light shone brightly. The light was the family's charm against the ghost. The girls had been talking to each other before falling asleep. All of a sudden a hazy brown shadow appeared at the bedroom doorway. The children would like to have jumped from the bed and run down the hallway, downstairs to their parents, but the form blocked their way.

The form came into the room and sat on the bed.

Was it the first Mrs. Beachy who showed herself as a shadowy figure to those children? Was it the first Mrs. Beachy who sat down at the foot of their bed, perhaps coming into the room out of habit to remind them to say their prayers?

Beachy had recently given the family notice and asked them to vacate the premises because he planned to marry - for the third time. This time he would marry a woman who had helped him at the auction, one with whom he had become close.

Yes, Beachy had planned to remarry and move his new wife into the white farmhouse. But Beachy was murdered.

Because of the nature of Beachy's death in the late spring of 1992, there was speculation among some that perhaps he might haunt the auction barn. And Mary? Would she continue to haunt the white farmhouse?

If both must remain earthbound for all eternity, why be separated? In 1995, heavy snow collapsed the roof of the former 522 Auction Barn. The area where Martin Beachy had met his end was completely crushed, as if the auctioneer's final gavel had slammed down on it. Locals saw a black humor in this and wondered if perhaps the spirit of Martin Beachy was now homeless.

The seasons pass. The finger fogs wind their way through the valley and enshroud the white farmhouse on Salem Road. The peepers sound their mating calls, shrill yet hollow throughout the swampy lowland. It seemed to some that Mary had called Martin home.

Big Brown George Row

"The big brown man is not coming after me. He is going to the barn to milk his cows, this man who slips out of the outside wall of the pantry and passes by the window of the kitchen door. He has a white face, a tired, long face, like someone getting up in the morning. That's how I know he is going to milk his cows. The birds are his cows, the mourning doves that have a lonesome moo like an unmilked cow."

Some 230 years ago, George Row, wearing a brown hat and collarless waistcoat, left his farm in Germany, boarded the British ship *Phoenix* in Rotterdam, Holland, and sailed to Philadelphia, where he took the oath of allegiance to the English Crown. He heard from his fellow Germans in the crowded city that there was good farm land to be had in the western frontier, so he obtained a warrant and survey and moved to Penn's Township, Northumberland County, with his wife, Mary, and three sons, George, John, and Martin. The 50 acres of valley land he bought turned out to be rich and fertile, and he named his plantation "Boat," perhaps in remembrance of the ship that had carried him across the Atlantic, or perhaps in ironic recognition of the aquifers and melting snows that spilled forth around his log home every early spring.

The mid 1770's was not a good time to move to northern central Pennsylvania. Although the Delaware, Shawnee, Conoy, Nanticoke, Munsee, and Mohican were apparently no longer upset by the Albany purchase of 1754, which had ceded lands west of the Susquehanna they occupied under the shelter of the Iroquois to the Penns, new tensions were arising in the region following the murder of 10 Indian men, women, and children by Frederick Stump and John Ironcutter at Bake Oven Hill, not far from Row's plantation.

Only a few years after he settled at "Boat," Row enlisted in a Battalion of the Northumberland County Militia. Stationed at Focht's Mill in the Buffalo Valley, he was fatally wounded by a revengeful Indian with a musket ball that pierced his breast. He was buried on the ridge near his home, in the cemetery behind the church in the village named for the Row family (now Salem Lutheran church in the village of Salem). His epitaph reads:

GEORGE ROW

born 1723

killed by Indians 1780

Der Tod Gewiss, ungewiss der Tag, die Stunde auch

Nie mand wiseen mag drum fuerchte. Erected 1890.

(Translation: Death is certain, the day is uncertain, and neither does one know the hour)

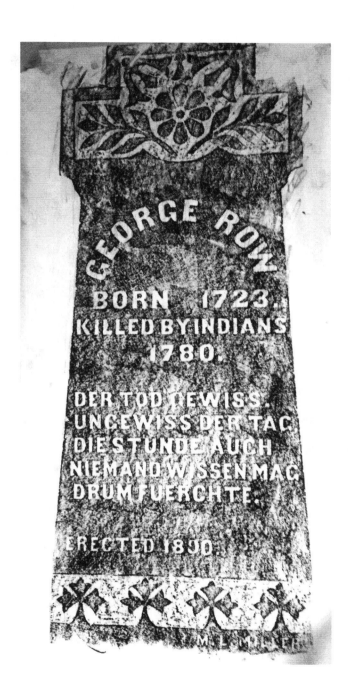

GEORGE ROW

BORN 1723.
KILLED BY INDIANS
1780.

DER TOD GEWISS.
UNGEWISS DER TAG.
DIE STUNDE AUCH
NIEMAND WISSEN MAG
DRUM FUERCHTE

ERECTED 1890.

Some 230 years later, my 7-year-old daughter is seeing a man, in a brown hat and collarless waistcoat, pass through the outside wall of our old log farmhouse and walk across the back porch.

"I wish we lived in a new house," she continues thinking, "with a garage where I can park my bike, and the chain won't rust. I ride to the end of the long lane, where the church and cemetery stick up over the hill, then I turn around and ride back. My mom has to drive me to Deborah's, to Amber's, to Jen's. Where the old barn has fallen down, she has tried to plant a garden in the shallow dirt. At night bats tumble from our roof like big black butterflies.

"If I can't live in a new house, then I wish I had my brother's room. His walls are white and crumbly, but he doesn't have an old stove pipe sticking out of his wall. The chimney covered in plaster hangs over my chest-of-drawers. I made my mom move my bed to the other wall. A plate covers the old stove pipe, a pretty woman picking roses. At night she is hidden in fog. I lie with the light on and wish I could run into my mom and dad's room.

"But the big brown man is not coming after me. His cows are calling him."

The Pow-Wower

When I was a young man about nineteen or twenty, and a student at Penn State, I developed a bad case of warts on the palm of my left hand. At the peak of their outbreak, the warts numbered about ten large ones, each with smaller satellite warts around them. They bulged up especially big at the base of my palm, spread humped across its entire expanse, bubbling up again furiously at the bottoms of my fingers, bulbous, bumptious, almost seething. They weren't painful, but they were certainly embarrassing -- to me, perhaps even more so to my parents. Whenever I was visiting them, mom and dad would at some point ask me, "How are your warts?" Frowning I'd hold out my hand to view, as if in confession of some infraction I had committed. They'd shake their heads and click their tongues, disturbed by the ugly sight, and perhaps also by the thought of the great activity that might have produced it, though if they ever suspected such a possible cause, they were tolerant people, and respectful enough of my privacy never to mention it.

Whether or not such activity actually caused the warts, refraining from it was out of the question for me. So I first attempted to disperse the fat rollicking fellows having a field day on my palm by dousing them with Compound W, the common wart-remover found in drugstores. I started using Compound W when the warts first appeared. But the salicylic acid solution only damaged the terrain, carving craters in the warts and leaving ridges and most of the mountain intact, and it did nothing to prevent more warts from mounding upward. One package of Compound W followed another, and I eventually gave up buying it. At the suggestion of a cousin of mine, mom next concocted a sulfur paste and applied it to my palm. But this did nothing more than stain my hand yellow, making the warts even more conspicuous, and she stopped the applications after a few trials. I got into the knack of hiding my left hand when I was around other people, keeping it under the table when I was sitting, stuffing it into my pocket while standing. When I was alone I'd stare at the warts, picking at the ones that had been damaged by the Compound W and, amazed at their tenacity, wondering why they couldn't just be dug out with tweezers or a pocket knife. Sometimes I almost grew to admire them, noting how the assemblage resembled a constellation of stars seen on a clear night.

"How are your warts?" mom and dad asked on my next vacation home.

I grimaced, holding open the palm of my hand.

My mom next made arrangements for me to visit a physician who was skilled in cryosurgery, a method of removing abnormal tissue by the application of extreme cold. Mom and I listened intently as the doctor explained to us what modern medicine knew about warts.

"We don't really know what causes warts. We know

they're caused by a type of virus, but we really don't know what brings on an onset of them."

He hunkered down at the table upon which I rested my upraised palm and picked up his cryo-gun, the tool with which he would seek to destroy the epithelial tumors by blasting them with liquid nitrogen.

"Don't worry. We'll get rid of these things for you."

I reached the age of twenty-one and graduated from college, all my warts still intact. I took a summer job at a sub shop to save up money to move to New York City in the fall, somehow managing to conceal my left palm while slicing tomatoes and luncheon meats and placing all those things in a bun. When the fall came, my plans to move to New York City fell through, and I made alternative plans to go to Boston. I had a vague idea of what I would do with my future, but my mom apparently thought that whatever that was it would be all the more difficult to carry out with so many warts on my hand. I can imagine her talking to her fellow teachers in the faculty room at the school where she taught:

"My son still has all those warts. I don't know what to do."

"Yes, he's certainly at the age where he should have outgrown them," one teacher said.

"Have you tried Compound W?" another teacher asked.

"We've tried Compound W and a sulfur concoction. A doctor has tried to freeze them off. We've tried everything. Nothing has worked."

The assistant principal, a well-educated, but culturally open-minded, man, suggested that perhaps a pow-wower should be consulted. He knew personally of one who had treated someone successfully for cancer.

"At this point, I'll try anything," my mom said.

Living in the central Susquehanna Valley, with its large population of Pennsylvania Germans, my parents and I had certainly heard of pow-wowing, although we (perhaps like most Pennsylvania Germans themselves) never had any personal experience with it. As I drove my mom's car to Trevorton, near where the pow-wower lived, I was curious to learn more about this practice of healing that the

American mainstream has relegated to the status of unreliable folk remedy, if not outright superstition.

The term "pow-wow," an appropriation of the Algonquian word for a spiritual gathering, was first used by John George Hohman in his 1819 book, *Pow-Wows or Long Lost Friend, A Collection of Mysterious and Invaluable Arts and Remedies* (a book I was not then familiar with). In the book, Hohman offers a collection of magical rituals and spells to deal with all kinds of ailments and other everyday problems: how "to prevent the Hessian fly from injuring wheat," how "to compel a thief to return stolen goods," how "to make chickens lay many eggs." His cure for a fever, for example, is as follows:

Write the following words upon a paper and wrap it up in knot-grass (breiten Megrieb), and then tie it upon the body of the person who has the fever:
Potmat Sineat,
Potmat Sineat,
Potmat Sineat.

Hohman seems to have been especially good at ridding a "wheal in the eye," as he lists the names of four people he cured of this problem. His testimonials, though, include cures for other ailments he effectively rendered: an ulcer on the leg, a severe pain in the arm, headaches, convulsions, "the wild-fire" on a sore cheek, and a burn from boiling coffee. He says this about the source of his knowledge:

This book is partly derived from a work published by

a Gypsy, and partly from secret writings, and collected with much pain and trouble, from all parts of the world, at different periods, by the author, John George Hohman. I did not wish to publish it; my wife, also, was opposed to its publication; but my compassion for my suffering fellow-men was too strong, for I had seen many a one lose his entire sight by a wheal, and his life or limb by mortification.

I found the dirt road up the hill to the trailer where the pow-wower lived. He was a wiry man with thinning brown hair. He wore browline eyeglasses, a dark-green plaid shirt, and, high on the waist, crisp, clean, dark blue jeans. His wife was doing the dishes in the kitchen. With no small talk except a perfunctory comment about the weather, he invited me to sit down on the sofa while he perched in an armchair close by. He took a quick look at my hand, then walked over to a closet, wandered into the kitchen, and came back with two halves of a potato. He rubbed each wart (or wart "expanse") three times with the exposed portion of one of the potato halves. Then he reached for the Holy Bible kept at hand on a folding table and read a verse or two, something or other about Jesus Christ and His Goodness.

"Now," he went on, "take this half a potato and bury it under an eave. Somewhere where the rain drips down. If the potato rots, your warts will go away. But if it sprouts, they won't."

"That makes sense," I said. "What about the other half?"

"My wife will probably use that for supper sometime."

I asked him how much I owed him for his services. He said there was no charge.

I went home and told my parents about the procedure. The next morning, my dad and I took a shovel and went into the back yard to bury the potato half under a leaky gutter. About a week later, I loaded up a U-Haul and set off for Boston, my mom breaking down in tears as she hugged me goodbye. A week or two after I settled into my new apartment at Inman Square, Cambridge, I received a Sunday phone call from my parents. When I finished telling them how my Portuguese landlord was a nice guy and was helping me wallpaper my kitchen and bedroom and that I had gotten a part-time job as a desk attendant at the YMCA, they asked me how my warts were doing.

"I'm glad you asked," I said. "They're completely gone."

Postscript: Hohman's cure for warts is slightly different from the cure I encountered from the Trevorton pow-wower. The idea of burial under the eaves is the same, but instead of a potato half, Hohman recommends rubbing the wart with roasted chicken-feet.

Ghosts of the Governor Snyder Mansion

Simon Snyder's last days were not happy ones. The sixty-year-old former governor now lived in the stone mansion he had built in 1816 in Selin's Grove, a small river town fifty miles north of the capital of Harrisburg, and he was still a busy man, overseer of the poor for Penn's Township and a state senator for Union County, formed out of Northumberland County in 1813. But as the old man looked out the third-story window of his house over the rooftops of the town founded by his brother-in-law Anthony Selin, his heart was troubled by domestic problems and financial worries. For the nine years he was Pennsylvania's first "Dutch" governor, championing the common man, seeing the state through the second war with England, calling for the establishment of public schools, he had neglected his own business affairs, his many landholdings, his grist mill and store.

He still had a lawsuit over his head: the heirs of his profligate brother John claimed that he and Anthony, as administrators of the estate, conspired to cheat them out of their inheritance. And just recently his eighteen-year-old son, Frederick, had died of typhoid. Simon could feel a sickness growing in his bones. Was the wobbling of the rooftops caused by a distortion in the window glass, or was it the fever starting to overtake him too?

Simon died of typhoid on November 9, 1819, a little more than a month after his son. The family buried the third governor of Pennsylvania, Selin's Grove's most distinguished citizen, in the cemetery of the Old First Lutheran Church a few blocks from his home, in a grave unmarked for seventeen years, then belatedly covered with a blank marble slab.

A hundred and fourteen years later the Governor Snyder's stone mansion is occupied by attorney Harry

Coryell and family. It is Halloween, and the heart of little, seven-year-old David Coryell, the lawyer's youngest son, is full of excitement and mischief. He and his older brother, Pierce, plan to scare their buddies: while David leads them out to the sidewalk in front of the mansion, Pierce will scoot up to the third floor, don dad's Knight Templar hat and hold a lighted candle, then prance in front of the windows pretending to be the ghost of Governor Snyder!

It is a night of fun and frolic: David and buddies bob for apples, play pin the tail on the donkey, see who can spit cider the farthest. Then at the appointed time David escorts his friends outside -- the prank is pulled off perfectly, the buddies scattering to the streets. Doubled over with laughter, David is soon joined by Pierce, giggling and out of breath. But the next moment David feels left alone in his merriment. He looks up at his suddenly quiet brother and follows the older boy's frightened eyes to the third-story window, where a hatless, handsome face is gazing out.

This story became the central feature of David Coryell's reminiscences fifty-three years later, recorded in his column, "My Childhood Paradise," in the Selinsgrove Times-Tribune. Coryell loved the old mansion he grew up in and which he retired to after a career in the park service, the grand federal-style structure, in the double parlor of which his parents took their marriage vows in 1917.

He was fascinated with its eerie elegance, the large stairway, the broad landings, the arched doorways, the huge rooms, the mysterious attic and the basement opening onto an outdoor terrace, once the Snyders' kitchen, with its large, open fireplaces with swinging cranes. He describes exploring its nooks and crannies, looking for secret rooms and passageways, tunnels that were supposedly part of the Underground Railroad, a sunken garden containing Indian artifacts, and a possible grave on the grounds, where one of Simon Snyder's servants supposedly made a deathbed wish to be buried.

The home in which Simon Snyder died, and which the eventually destitute Snyder family continued to own until 1864, was a place of strange happenings: sudden gusts of winds on the dates Snyder family members died, soft music, peculiar odors, muffled crying -- and the face in the attic window.

Diane was not aware of Coryell's Halloween experience when she lived in the rectory of the Episcopal Church next door to the mansion and one night was walking by the mansion with her husband. She happened to look up at the third-story window -- the mansion was lit by spotlights and the window was an attractive architectural item that could easily draw anyone's attention -- and saw there the clear image of a face of a man, clear enough that she recognized it as the handsome and dignified mien of Simon Snyder from portraits in history books. The face was not laughing or crying, but bore an intense stoical expression. She pointed it out to her husband -- he didn't see anything. The couple dipped their heads, circled around the sidewalk to view the window at different angles. The face remained gazing intently, overlooking Diane, until, not knowing what else to do, the couple went home.

She saw the face a couple times after that, while she lived at the rectory in late 1988 and early 1989, and only later came across Coryell's account of his and his brother's experience in 1933.

Simon Snyder's corpse lay beneath a blank marble slab when, in 1855, a new county was formed out of Union County and named in honor of the area's most distinguished citizen. The corpse remained in a nameless grave for another thirty years, until the state legislature in 1885 erected a monument at the site, topped with a bust of the Governor. In the fall of 2003, a store in town displayed a photograph of the monument in its front window. Someone had placed an orange highway construction cone on top of the head, so the Governor, supporter of public education, looked like a classroom dunce.

When Diane saw the Governor's face in the window, the Coryells no longer owned the mansion, which in 1978 was entered in the State and National Registry of Historical Places. The real estate had been bought by an out-of-town couple, Ann and Tom McNabb, who have turned the mansion into a charming gift shop. Among the appurtenances of the purchase, in addition to some horseshoes and a cannonball passed down by the Coryells, is the legend of the Governor's ghost, with reports that Simon's otherworldly presence adds a pleasant aroma to the smells of potpourri and scented candles otherwise available at the shop.

Several years after the McNabbs hung out their signs, their daughter, Heather, and her husband, Steven Leason, moved into the basement, scrubbed the floors and the Governor's original fireplaces, and opened up a brew pub, offering delicious food, a smoke-free atmosphere, and a variety of award-winning homemade beers. Though the McNabbs are pleased with their purchase of an apparition, a quaint addition to their establishments, apparently no one in the family has seen a ghost. The same cannot be said about at least one of the employees and a couple of the customers.

Scott (last name withheld) began tending bar for Steve and Heather in January of the year they opened up.

"The old man who used to live there would come in every now and then," the affable Scott tells me over the phone. "He'd always ask me, 'Have you seen anything yet?' I always had to tell him, 'No.' "

Then on a warm August evening, as Scott was cleaning up the bar and preparing to tell the last remaining customers out in the garden that they'd have to leave, he saw an S-shaped wisp of smoke curling beneath a lamp by the fireplace.

"It was kind of like a wig, or the back of someone's grey head of hair."

Swooning with goose bumps, he turned around to do some paperwork, but could not shake away the appearance, over his right shoulder, of another shoulder, bearing a buckskin jacket.

"When I jerked around, there was nothing there. And then I was out of there. I mean, I didn't even bother finishing with the paperwork. I didn't turn out the lights. I didn't tell the customers they had to leave. I just dropped everything and bolted."

A few nights later, when "the old man who used to live there" came in for an oatmeal stout, Scott told him that he had, indeed, finally seen something.

"Oh yeah," the patron leaned forward, smiling. "Was it the guy in a Confederate uniform or the guy in a buckskin jacket?"

Scott grew accustomed to the figure in deer hide, even dubbing him "George," the name the Loony Tunes' Abominable Snowman calls Bugs Bunny. Though the apparition is accompanied by an icy cold feeling and the smell of manure, Scott got in the habit of saying goodbye to him every night when he closed bar. He has seen George, out of the corner of his eye, more than a dozen times.

"Has anyone else seen him?" I ask over the phone.

"Two people I can remember. A young lady in her 30's was sitting at the bar. Said George was looking right into her eyes. She left the bar in tears. Then there was another guy in his mid 20's. He liked to drink a lot, and I would have to sometimes cut him off. One night he was saying, 'Oh, there's no such thing.' Then someone told him to sit a few bar stools down, where no one was sitting because it felt icy cold there. He sat there for a few minutes then started crying out, 'Tell him to get away from me.' Finally he got up and said, 'I'm not coming back.' I didn't see either of those two customers afterwards."

(A ghost in a restaurant, I think to myself, is generally good for business. But, as restaurant owners and employees have told me, you can't please everyone, all of the time.)

Scott left the employment of the brew pub in July of this year, but not, he emphasizes, because he didn't like working there or because he was disturbed by things in his periphery of vision. Now he goes to the brew pub socially, and fraternizing with friends and acquaintances on the other side of the bar, he no longer sees George.

"Do you miss him?" I ask.

"Definitely," he laughs.

Mother's Helper

Georgie was seventeen when she and some high school friends vacationed in Canada. She had just graduated from Shikellamy High School in Sunbury, Pennsylvania, and like most of her friends wore her class ring with pride. The day she lost it she was heartbroken. She and some friends had taken the rowboat out on the small lake where they were staying. As they paddled around the center of the lake, Georgie let her arm hang over the side and trawled the cool, deep water with her open hand.

"Oh, no! My ring!" She felt the heavy gold ring slip from her finger and watched in horror as it disappeared into the depths of the dark green water. There was no way to retrieve the precious item. The lake at the spot they had been boating was far too deep for anyone to go in after it. It was gone. Lost in a lake in Ontario, Canada.

A few years later Georgie got married and after a time had a little baby girl. She and her young husband rented an old brick country house in Union County several miles from her family home in Sunbury. The house stood alone on County Line Road between Snyder County and Union County just down the road from Blue Hill. Each morning when her husband went off to work she stayed home with the baby. She did not have a car and with a new baby and few visitors, many hours were spent watching afternoon soap operas and game shows as she sat on the sofa in the living room. Some housebound mothers might have felt isolated and lonely but not Georgie. She had company, spirit company. When they first moved into the house Georgie often caught sight of a woman in black that strolled through the back yard each day. As long as the woman was outside and Georgie "looked at her through glass," she could see her quite plainly. She knew the woman was a spirit because the figure tended to come and go, appear and disappear before her eyes. As if by special invitation one day the spirit woman came into the house to visit.

"I was sitting on the sofa holding the baby and all of a sudden I saw a dark hazy mass come into the room. I knew it was the woman because it had the shape of the woman from the yard, but it was all fuzzy like she was out of focus or something. I had a rocking chair by the window but usually sat on the sofa to watch TV. I watched the shape as she glided across the living room. Then she just SAT DOWN!"

The visit became routine. After Georgie's husband left for work each day and the breakfast dishes were cleared, Georgie found her place on the sofa and in came the lady to sit all afternoon in her place in the rocking chair by the window. As soon as her husband's car pulled into the driveway at suppertime and Georgie heard his key in the lock, heard the door open and heard the door close, the lady disappeared, once again only to be spotted through the window glass walking around the back yard.

"She never left until she heard that door close and heard him call my name. Then WHOOSH! She'd be gone! Back into the yard. I never did see her face. She kept her head covered with a shawl. But I could see her very plainly just like she was really there."

A few years later the landlady of the house on County Line Road decided to sell the place and Georgie and her husband were told that they would need to move. They did. The new owners took occupancy and had lived in the house for several years when one day Georgie got a call from her previous landlady.

"Georgie," she said. "I have something that may belong to you. You must have left it in the old house when you moved out. The tenant called and said she found it on the windowsill in the living room. Odd thing, you know. She has lived in the house for a while now and she says she must have cleaned that sill a hundred times. Never saw it before. She doesn't know where it came from but we think it's yours."

"What did she find?" Georgie asked.

"A ring. A class ring from Shikellamy High School. Blue stone. Class of '71. What were your initials back then?"

"GLH."

"That's it – and with the initials GLH inside."

As Georgie drove up to her former home to retrieve her long lost class ring she said she knew who had brought the ring back for her from Canada perhaps as a gift, perhaps as just a little way of letting Georgie know that although she was missed she was not forgotten by her live-in spirit companion during her quiet days on County Line Road.

"One more thing," Georgie adds with a big smile. "It was Mother's Day."

Penn's Tavern

Illustration by John Johnson

She must have had a bad day.

The customers had left the tavern for the night and the help sat around the bar relaxing, talking, counting tips and folding napkins. Drinks were on the house – the stout German beer flowed freely. September can be a busy month for a restaurant that specializes in German-American food. One of the staff got up to use the lady's room. The door was locked. Someone else must be in there, she thought, and went back to the bar to sit down. Five minutes passed and she got up again, walked across the wide plank floors, and tried the iron latch – still locked. The lock was a simple one – a basic hook and latch on the inside of the door. It still signaled "occupancy" and preserved privacy. The woman sat down at the bar again to wait. Another minute – back to the lady's room door, jiggled the latch – still locked.

"OK – who's missing? Who's in the lady's room all this time," she called out to anyone, to everyone. In a very businesslike manner the head waitress set the napkin she was folding aside, reached across the bar to grab a flat knife and walked to the locked door.

"Did that thing lock itself again?" she asked as she poked the blade through the crack in the doorframe, popped the hook up. The door swung open. Empty.

"What do you mean - again?"

"Humph," she shook her head. "I don't know why – but it's the seventh time today that the door had locked itself – from the inside."

A long time ago, legend has it, a woman died in what is now the kitchen area of Penn's Tavern. Penn's Tavern is located about 7 miles south of Sunbury on Route 147. To reach it, one must cross the railroad tracks. It sits along the Susquehanna River in a town known as Fisher's Ferry. The tavern reputedly built in 1703 was at one time the hosting place for travelers along the river and the eastern house for those crossing the river and using the ferry. It has been during its lifetime mainly an eating and lodging establishment though at certain points it has been a home to different families. The building is made of field stone, floors and beams darkened by age are made of broad pine planks and beams. At different times, the stone has been covered with plaster, paneling, wallpaper, and paint. Broad plank pine, considered a poor man's floor at various times during its history, was most often covered up, as is plywood today. Ah! But the stories those planks could tell of the people who have strode across them, or stood on them to stand at the bar, look out a window or hold the gaze of another in their eyes.

The most well-known story of the tavern is about the grandson of William Penn. As it is told, although William Penn was a fair, honest and humble man he had two sons, John and Thomas, who weren't. John Penn had a son also named John. John Penn the elder and his wife lived in both Pennsylvania and England. Their wealth in the colonies gave them a certain status that they felt put them above the common folk. At seventeen years old, young John met a young woman, Mary Cox, and as only a seventeen-year-old boy can do, fell desperately in love with her.

Mary came from a poor working class family, however. She was "not good enough" for a Penn as far as John's parents were concerned and they set forth to discourage the relationship. John would have none of their meddling and set sail with bride to be in arm across the English Channel to France where he married her. He then set sail for the colonies. Shortly after landing in

Philadelphia, Mary was kidnapped! By Indians! She was taken into the woods, Penn's Woods, if you like, and disappeared from John Penn's life. After seven years she was presumed dead and he remarried. Another eight years passed. Mary was not dead. She escaped from her captors and made her way across the ridges, through the tangled briars and brush and the deep virgin forest to the banks of the Susquehanna River. She found the stone building that served the area. The years of living outside of civilization had taken their toll. She was dying.

The proprietors of the tavern took pity on the woman and gave her a comfortable bed in which to die. The room was just off the main meeting area, which is now the main dining room at the current Penn's Tavern. Destined to meet once again, the lovers were united when John Penn stopped into the tavern for a night's lodging. The commotion surrounding the woman from the forest who had found her way to the tavern to die in comfort caught John's attention. He was told what was happening. That a woman, Mary Cox was her name, had escaped a long captivity by Indians and had found her way to the tavern. Realizing that this was indeed his first wife, he gathered her up in his arms and the story has it, she died, united with her husband. She was buried about a mile north of the tavern in an old colonial cemetery that sits above the banks of the river.

Because the story is so well known among locals, it is presumed that the ghost – or at least one of them – is the ghost of Mary Cox. The woman in blue. Workmen have reported seeing a woman wearing a blue dress gazing at them from the window of the tavern – when the tavern is supposed to be empty. Or is she the woman in red?

Told as a firsthand account by a former waitress of the tavern, there was a night when after all the customers had left that she stepped into the main dining room to see an elegantly dressed woman wearing a dark red dress standing in the far corner of the room. The woman appeared to be looking for something. Christy assumed that she was a customer and perhaps had left something behind. "May I help you?" she asked, at which point the women just disappeared. "Faded right before my eyes," Christy recalls. "One minute she was there – she was most definitely there! And the next – she was just – gone!"

A local woman tells this story:

One night she stopped into the tavern to buy a couple of six-packs. It was an evening during the week, during the summer, and for whatever reason there was no one seated either at the bar or at any of the tables. As she approached the long, heavily varnished oak bar she saw four men standing in the kitchen. They were talking loudly, laughing and drinking. They were also dressed in the costumes of soldiers. The clothes were dusty, dirty, and very worn looking. One of the men was dressed as an officer and seemed to be controlling the conversation. Thinking to herself that they must be a theater group, she patiently waited for the bartender to appear. He did not. Neither did any of the men in the kitchen seem to notice her. Best to get their attention.

"Excuse me..." she said. Immediately the conversation ceased. The lead man looked at her and he looked shocked. The other men turned to look at her. Then they just disappeared. Poof!

At a recent auction the present owner bought back the original bar that was used during the Civil War era. Fisher's Ferry is only about a hundred miles north of Gettysburg, PA. One can only imagine the conversations that took place at the tavern during that troubled time in our history. A curious thought, however, is this: If this woman was able to see these "ghosts" or images of the past and as it seems, they were able to see her, an image from the future – are those conversations still taking place? Do current customers and workers wander through and among past customers and employees?

One employee of the tavern it seems has never left, and not because of any emotional trauma that may have occurred while he was alive. He just seems to have liked his job at the tavern while he was alive. Being dead was no reason to quit working or playing.

Regulars know the character as the handyman. Some time during the early nineteenth century a man lived and worked at the tavern. He was of the common German desent that dominates the area. He may have even been from Germany. His name has been lost. Around 1992 a psychic visited the tavern and found the "hotspot" for the handyman to be near the fireplace in the main dining room.

Perhaps one of his many jobs was to keep the fire burning. During the crisp autumn evenings and long winter nights many a tankard of ale was downed, many a story told and many a song sung. The rowdier the patrons got, the better the handyman is said to have enjoyed himself. He still enjoys himself.

Illustration by John R. Johnson

In late summer of 2001, a group of ghost hunters came to the tavern in hopes of, if not spotting a spirit, at least getting a good picture of one. After wandering around the place and finding various hotspots for spirit activity, they wondered if perhaps different types of music might conjure up more than just a good mood. They asked the house musicians, a fiddler and piano player, to play "something French." Penn's Tavern is not from Dauphin County where many French had settled at one time. The signals were weak. They then asked for "some music from the Civil War." It's a wonder soldiers from the kitchen didn't manifest in full color and uniform for that, but at best, the ghost hunters managed to photograph a few orbs and the needles on the magnet meters jumped quite a bit. Then they asked "for some old German stuff."

The handyman must have sung "Auch Du Lieber, Augustine" many a night as he stoked the fire. Caught on digital cameras, orbs and lights abounded over the heads of both musicians and literally danced in the air above the fireplace. The most astounding evidence of the existence of "the handyman," however, showed up later in a hard film photograph. Floating above the fiddler's head, in a smoky looking cloud that had not appeared in real life, is the unmistakable image of a very happy old man, mountaineer's hat with its downturned brim shadowing his eyes, but his mouth broad and grinning at the music makers. On seeing the photo one gets the feeling that given one more verse of music for a warm-up the handyman would have joined right in on the chorus, gravelly voice singing away in old German as he may have done a hundred and some odd years ago.

For a building that has been around for so long -- it is, after all, the oldest building in Northumberland County – there are nights when one can sit at the bar, look at the patrons and feel as if a group of interlopers from another era have chosen to come together for an evening of camaraderie. It is a moody place, an emotional place, where even strangers feel as if they have just walked into a gathering to which they were personally invited. Considering the plethora of spirits that continue to gather at the tavern – perhaps they were.

The Phantom Fiddler of Paddy Mountain

There is a story told in Centre County about a spirit fiddler who was killed by a rattle snake and haunts the top of Paddy Mountain. This is a fictionalized account of what may have happened...

Tie a fiddle string to your big toe and you'll be a good dancer.

Always borrow rosin. Never use your own or you'll get your fiddle in trouble

Wear a ring of ash twigs round your neck and snakes won't get ya'.

If a rattlesnake bites you, tease it till it bites itself then follow it to the special snakeweed. Eat some and you'll be cured. 'Course if one bites you and no amount of teasing makes it mad enough to bite itself you might want to get all the snakes in the vicinity fighting amongst themselves. Then just follow them all to the snakeweed.

Brazilwood is a known snake chaser. If you're going to fiddle in snake country, make sure your bow is made of it.

Jack knew all of this stuff. He made it his business to know. In fact most of the folks in his family knew everything a fiddler in the eastern mountains needed to know. For as far back as anyone could remember there had been fiddlers in Jack's family. Whether what Jack knew and his family knew was mostly true or truly true was of no real matter to him, though. Best to pocket all the bits of knowledge about fiddling and living in the hills just to be on the safe side.

Jack's stomping grounds lay several ridges from the river in the mountains. It is wild and rough terrain. Loose stones and slippery evergreen needles are ready to trip anyone trying to climb the steep hills. The tangled roots of

49

wind-fell trees grab at many a poor soul who attempts to slide down a muddy embankment to a stream. In past times the woods had been alive with wolves, bison, snakes, and panthers. Now just the deer, bear, elk and snakes remained.

Mountain winters are harsh, cold and colorless. Spring, when it does come, takes its sweet time in setting the blossoms on the dogwood and in coaxing the leaves from the branches of the black walnut, red oak and ash trees. Once summer arrives, however, all that had once seemed hesitant to show itself, vines out, branches out, and leafs out till a traveler in the woods can hardly find his feet, let alone his way.

Jack never lost his way in the woods. He knew all the trails, paths and streams to follow to get from one side of the mountain to the other, from one dance to the other. He knew his way quite well up to the top of Paddy Mountain and had a special rock where he could sit and play his fiddle all night just for himself if he desired. When he was up there all the folks in the hollows could hear him, so it was for them as well that he played. But you wouldn't catch them following Jack up the mountain, fiddle strings tied around their big toes ready to dance to Jack's tunes. They knew better. The hilltop was inhabited by a large family of timber rattlers and was best avoided.

Jack was greatly afraid of ghosts and spirits but had no fear of the creatures that lived in the woods. He was well acquainted with the curious glowing eyes of the critters that peeped out from behind a log or a tangle of monkey vine. He took great pleasure in coaxing them closer to listen to his music. Even Paddy Mountain's family of rattlers would glide out from beneath the rocks and fallen leaves, keeping their distance, mind you, hypnotized by the sweet sounds of his fiddle. They never bit him. Of course, the fact that he made sure to wear his ash twig necklace, use his Brazilwood bow and his borrowed rosin, not store-bought block, might have accounted for this. Jack took great care when he fiddled amongst the snakes of Paddy Mountain. He'd heard a story about a fiddler in Tennessee who still haunted the spot where rattlers had done him in and Jack had no intention of becoming a phantom fiddler. That guy did everything wrong. Jack did everything right. He never harmed his slithery, rattling audience. He charmed them.

Jack believed that the moon as well as the animals liked his music. As the story goes one particular night when the Hunter's Moon rose big and orange, an eerily suspended Jack o' Lantern, its cockeyed grin and winking eye, peeking between the ridges, Jack tipped his hat to the golden orb, took his fiddle and bow from the wall where they hung, stuffed a block of rosin in his back pocket and headed up the mountain, dried leaves crunching beneath his bare feet. After a spell, the soft strains of Jack's fiddle drifted down like finger fogs into the hollows. The hill folks thought he was crazy for fiddling where he was, amongst the rattlers, but Jack was Jack and they liked his music. The smiling moon rode to the top of the sky dome. Jack went from one tune to the other with nary a pause in between notes. The moon rose to its high point and started down the other side. Jack played on. Midnight came and went. Jack played on. At dawn the western hills swallowed the grinning but satisfied moon whole, and Jack played on. Even as the songs of the morning birds and the cackling, egg-laying hens ate his notes, he played. He didn't stop. The hill folks scratched their heads and worried a bit when noon came and he was still fiddling.

"What's up with old Jack?"

"It's not like him to go 'round all the tunes he knows and start repeating them."

"He's fourth time on 'Turkey In the Straw.'"

"He hates to play 'Orange Blossom Special' and he's run that train 'round the track a dozen times since he started fiddling last night."

"Chicken Reel – two dozen!"

"Maybe someone ought to go up there and give him a tap."

"Yep. Maybe his needle's stuck."

"Why don't you go up there and see if he needs help?"

"No way! All them rattlers 'round his feet! Not me!"

Jack kept on fiddling. The sun came up; the sun went down. The moon rose and set, rose and set, till it tired of Jack's obnoxious repetition of tunes and disappeared altogether. Jack kept fiddling. By now the folks were really worried. His fiddling was starting to sound a might tattered. "Probably wore his fingers down to stumps," they mused. But no one ventured up the mountain. His strings wore thin and popped – first the E, then the A, then the G, which was pretty old to start with - till all he had was the D string left. As each string popped off, it wrapped itself around Jack's big toe and he began to dance. He kept on fiddling. One by one each hair on his bow snapped and was carried away by the cold autumn wind till he was fiddling with just the stick! He kept on.

Jack was fiddling for his life.

He had messed up royally. Sometime during a go-around at "Devil's Dream" his neck charm had begun to chafe and he tossed it into the weeds. The snakes slithered close. No problem, Jack thought. His bow was made of "gen-u-ine Brazilwood." That's what the guy at the flea market had told him when he sold him that along with the "gen-u-ine Stradivarius." His fiddle might be down to one string but it wasn't in any real trouble. The borrowed rosin took care of that. Or did it?

"Dang!' Jack sputtered to himself as he spied the block at his feet. "It's the light stuff!" Jack always bought the light stuff for lending, but made a point of borrowing the dark stuff. His toes were tapping like mad and with nothing decent to keep the snakes at bay, they moved in closer till they were right under his feet. Jack's foot dancing irritated them greatly and they rattled their rattlers at him to try to tell him to knock it off, but Jack took their rattling as requests for more tunes and fiddled more.

Although many a snake might be charmed by the sound of a fiddle, they don't take really well to being danced upon. If rattling a warning didn't work, maybe a little nip would. Grandpappy rattler was forced to chomp down. Knowing that fiddling usually charmed snakes into complacency, Jack found this curious. He fiddled some more. Grandmamma snake chomped down. He fiddled some more and his feet danced some more. This greatly irritated the snakes and one after another the family members chomped on Jack's toes in an effort to make him stop his dang fiddling so he'd quit dancing on them - aside from which at this point he sounded awful. Paganini might have been able to pull off playing a whole tune on one string, but Jack never strayed off first position so he didn't have much to work with.

Jack knew he was in serious trouble on account of all the bites, but also knew that if he could just get one snake to bite another all he had to do was follow it to the snakeweed, eat some and he'd be cured. And don't you know! Just when a couple of the kid rattlers had got riled up fighting for position to take a nip at old Jack and were fixing to take a nip at each other, his last string snapped! That was it. The music stopped. Jack's feet quit tapping. The snakes breathed a great sigh of relief, said "Good day," to one another, slithered back into their holes, albeit a little worse for the wear of Jack's infernal dancing, and settled in for a long winter's nap. And Jack – well, poor old Jack.

The hill folks say that if you have the nerve to pull on your snake boots, tie on your neck charm, climb up Paddy Mountain on the night of the full Hunter's Moon and sit down on Jack's rock, you will not hear him fiddling. Which is a good thing! Although Jack may still haunt the hilltop clutching his busted fiddle, busted is the way the snakes like it! They are much happier when he just sits there.

(Author's note: And I've been to Paddy Mountain and I listened for Jack's fiddling and I didn't hear a thing – so I figure this story to be true!)

The Headless Dog

A cat has its sharp claws, a horse its pummeling legs, a bear its giant paws. We admire the taut body of a dog, with its capacity to leap and run, but what the bicyclist fears about the beast snarling at his wheels is all in the head -- the salivating teeth, the powerful jaws. So it's curious that one of the most frightening apparitions to emerge in the Susquehanna Valley is an animal that would seem to pose no harm at all -- a headless dog.

The legend has been recorded in the historical annals of Snyder County. The late Foster Kreamer, a man noted for his truthfulness, has told local historians that when he was a boy he was attending a revival meeting at the Fisher's Schoolhouse, west of Rolling Green Park. He and another boy were standing on either side of the door, when a huge coal-black dog, sans tête, walked between them and sauntered through the door. Kreamer's friend was so overcome with fear that he sprinted at breakneck speed to his home nearby, but Kreamer, who had no place to run, dauntlessly entered the building. There, he could find no dog, and when he asked the people inside about it, no one had seen it.

The Fisher's Schoolhouse has recently been an ice cream parlor, where drivers and bicyclists on the back roads could stop for refreshments. If the headless dog haunted the place then, it was undoubtedly a very frustrated canine, unable to steal licks from little children's cones.

Despite its most recent appearance in Monroe Township, Snyder County, the brainless mastiff has mostly haunted the High Hill in Penn Township, a ridge just north of the Selinsgrove Center which runs from Hill End, along Route 204, to Fair Oaks, a crossroads north of the village of Salem.

The High Hill has long been noted to have been

werful Indian sorcery. This ridge and the
ɔf it, from which rise the water towers of the
ɔ Center, form a wedge-like valley known as the
Triangle, which was once a valuable hunting
gɪʊ for the Delaware and the Shawnee. These tribes, who lived here under the shelter of the Iroquois, who claimed the land in dealings with the colonial authorities, lost it as their hunting ground when the Iroquois ceded it to the Penns under the Albany Purchase of 1754. Disgruntled because they were unrepresented in the land negotiations, the Delaware and Shawnee attacked white settlers along Penn's Creek from Kratzerville, just north of the High Hill, to New Berlin, an event well remembered in Pennsylvania historical chronicles as the Penn's Creek Massacre.

Opposite the High Hill, on the east side of Penns Creek, it is said that a band of traveling Iroquois (no longer having free access to the Bloody Triangle) stole a big hog from a farm later owned by Clair Kratzer, then carried it further east to a farm owned by Norman D. App. There, they roasted it under a huge tree and, with conspicuous merriment and revelry gorged themselves in a sumptuous feast. Since then, every year on Christmas night, an eerie shriek has been heard echoing the entire length of the High Hill. It is claimed to be the blood-chilling death yell of an Indian warrior, dashing ferociously through the forests of the Bloody Triangle.

It is here, along the ridge of the screaming Indian, that the headless dog has most often appeared. Men walking along Fair Oak road at night have reported seeing it cross the road, and without a sound, ascend the steep bank of High Hill, pitched at 70-80 degrees. Sometimes its black massive bulk has been seen in a huge oak tree, the amorphous mass of fur rattling the branches with an unholy racket.

One night, Maria Stahl, an elderly woman who lived in a house later owned by Mrs. William Bingaman, was returning home from a visit with Hiram Smith. Her steps led her by the oak tree, and as she passed under its dark crown, a heavy, awkward being dropped down upon her back and flung its furry limbs around her neck. She struggled to toss it off, struggled to run -- the black shapeless thing kept its strangling grip upon her. Fortunately her house was nearby, and she managed to collapse, out of breath, against her gate. The ungainly burden suddenly released its hold upon her and disappeared. She was never able to give an accurate description of its appearance, but she was sure that it would have killed her had she not reached home.

Another time, a man was bicycling home in the moonlight, when just as he came upon the oak tree, his passage was blocked by a huge dog standing in the middle of the road. This creature seemed to have a head, but the man immediately recalled the stories of the headless dog -- and became uncannily frightened -- when the beast leapt onto the hill and scuffled up the leaf-littered bank, without a sound.

Related to the legend of the headless dog and the screaming Indian of High Hill is the belief long held by dwellers along the ridge that the mountain contains a buried treasure. The early Pennsylvania German settlers did not always have recourse to a bank in which to place their valuables, and the rural folk especially did not trust the few banking institutions that did exist, so the wise farmers often buried their savings in some secluded spot in the ground, sometimes placing a curse or hex upon the hoard to prevent any theft of their secreted cash. Having long heard of rumors of buried money on High Hill, a group of locals in 1940 hired a diviner from the coal regions who, with a divining rod of witch hazel, located a spot on the ridge he claimed to be chocked full of metal. The locals proceeded to the spot shortly after, at night, only to find the place "verhexed." Having dug two shallow feet, they were suddenly besieged by the sound of a million buzzing insects swarming about their heads. They picked up their shovels and ran off, crying, "The woods is full of devils."

Could there be a connection between the headless dog, the buried treasure, and the shrieking Indian of High Hill? Perhaps there is, if one considers that one cannot walk today at night along Fair Oak Drive without stirring up a barking dog from every farmhouse. A dog, with a head, is the guardian of property, and especially in the days when the white settlers lived uneasily upon their lands, the guardian of life, warning of the approach at night of an angry people who had not yet left the land. But a silent dog is a useless dog, a helpless dog, a dog that cannot keep at bay the silent approach of stifling death.

Perhaps, also, the buried treasure on High Hill is the dog's. Perhaps it is nothing but the bones from the huge hog roasted on the farm of Norman App, pushed by the dog to the hill, then pushed into the hole the dog had pawed up. And the poor canine is doomed forever to roam the hill without being able to get back its treasure -- unable to catch the scent of where the bones are buried.

But there is also a naturalistic explanation for the death yell of High Hill, and perhaps even for the strange animal that pounced upon Maria Stahl from the oak tree. I myself live near the ridge, at its western end, in an old log home on lands once owned by George Row, in the very midst of the Bloody Triangle, and later owned by Martin Beachy, the Amish antique dealer who was murdered at his auction barn and about whom rumors have circulated that he had buried old valuable coins on his property. Quite frequently at night, in the fall and early winter, I have heard horrible shrieks in the sparsely populated hills -- screams like a woman being attacked. For a long time I thought they were the sounds of a dying animal, perhaps a starving deer. Then my wife pointed out to me the following passage from Christy Ann Hensler's *Guide to Indian Quillworking*:

During the breeding season [roughly September through January], porcupines can emit the most blood-curdling screams ever heard in the wild....

But I have also heard sounds from the hills for which

I have no naturalistic explanation. Not long ago, the Eastern Delaware Nation, an association of people from Pennsylvania who claim Delaware ancestry, was considering leasing the vacated farmland of the Selinsgrove Center, which is most of the Bloody Triangle, for meeting grounds and historical preservation. The plans were never realized, but while they were still being made, I spoke several times with the people who were trying to negotiate the lease. One night, after such a conversation, while I was taking out the trash, I heard, coming from somewhere in the hills, so distinctly that I could not dismiss them as unreal, the lilting notes of an Indian flute, whimsical and joyous.

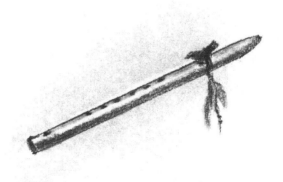

The White Woman of Montgomery's Bar

Montgomery's Bar is located just a few miles north of the junction of the north and west branches of the Susquehanna River. The area used to be known as "Shamokin" by the Indians. "Shamokin" translates as "where the eels live." There used to be very good eel fishing in the river at this junction. A large dam that was put up by a power company diverted the eels' opportunity to return to their spawning grounds in the Sargasso Sea, however. So there are no more eels here. Oddly enough the town near the dam is now named Shamokin Dam or if translated back from its original Native name, the "where the eels live" dam. But they don't live there anymore.

One town at the junction of the two branches is known as Northumberland and at one time was slated to become the capital of Pennsylvania. It was thought that a town on two rivers would support good commerce. As it is, the Susquehanna River is temperamental - floods or droughts wreak havoc on the levels of the river. Susquehanna in the Native language means, "muddy waters." It is high in the spring, low in the summer, and frozen in the winter. Back in the lumber era of Pennsylvania during the latter part of the nineteenth century it was common practice to use the waters of the river to carry the logs from the northern reaches of the

Commonwealth to the Chesapeake Bay and beyond. It was the raftsmen who performed this dangerous task. Balanced on the logs and flat boats they steered through strong currents of the spring flood season as a way of getting the logs to market.

For amusement and after a day's work was done, they often stopped at one of the many taverns along the banks of the muddy Susquehanna for a good drink, some dancing, and some music and to meet a pretty girl. A fiddler most often carried the music to the taverns. As they say, at that time the woods were full of fiddlers.

It happens - and this is a true story - that one evening at Montgomery's Bar the local young people had got together for a night of fun and frolic at the tavern which is now long gone, barely a stone left to mark where it once stood. One of the raftsmen, who remains nameless, often played his fiddle at this stop and set the folks to dancing with his wildly provocative tunes. Ah! But one night while he stood fiddling away for the dancers he spied a fair young maiden, a waitress and a beauty, in the crowd that filled the tavern. Not wanting to miss an opportunity to meet her and perhaps win her heart, he handed his fiddle over to a fellow rafts man who also happened to play the fiddle (as I said - the woods were full of them!) and wove his way across the room to meet Susan Hilbish.

Picture the scene as if it were taking place today and the rock musician and the dance for the teens and the waitress and the flattery that begets one when the Star of the show wants to meet you! Well, there you have Susan.

So they got it on, so to say. The fiddler and the waitress had a fine time dancing, and later on in conversation, and later on... Susan fell in love.

But the fiddler had to leave the next morning and finish guiding the logs to the end of the Susquehanna. He said he would be back - when the river ran right again for floating logs downstream. It took a year but Susan waited.

He did indeed come back to the tavern at

Montgomery's Bar. The young people once again danced to his wild fiddle music and Susan once again brought them their drinks and food, all the time sneaking a glance at the fiddler with whom she had fallen in love. But he did not see her in the crowd this time! No! As fickle as the river down which he had come, so was his heart! The year before he had been flooded with passion for Susan and now his passion for her was but a puddle on some muddy rocks. He saw yet another fair young maiden in the crowded tavern and handing his fiddle over once again to a river mate, he took off after a new girl.

Susan was crushed. Brokenhearted. Dispirited. She slowly crept up the stairs of the tavern and found her way into a closet to cry her tears for the fiddler in private. She scratched a poem about love lost on the wall of the closet.

Oh Faithless one, how little can you know

Of heartaches and pains that I endure

I loved you, trusted and in vain did wait

For the day when our love would be secure

But another heart now wins over mine,

My dreams of hope and love and life are gone

Be true to her, I pray, my dying wish

I end it all...

-Susan Hilbish

Then she took a bottle of poison and drank it. The words remained there for as long as the tavern stood.

Although the walls of the tavern no longer stand, the young people say that there is still a weeping that can be heard if one frequents the grounds of Montgomery's Bar. Every now and then one will claim to have seen a white mist in the shape of a woman hovering around tables that are no longer there. But the fiddler, who had promised Susan he would one day return to love her, has disappeared for good.

Trailer – Free! Will Deliver!

The old saying, "You get what you pay for," might apply in this case.

Sometime during the eighties, Cristi's parents were vacationing at a friend's house in upstate New York with some friends. At a point, an acquaintance of the friend stopped in and asked if the family might have need of a large three-bedroom house trailer in good shape. Well, they couldn't afford such a luxury at that time but a better home than they were living in would certainly be nice. No problem, said the acquaintance. The trailer was free – free to become a good home. Yes, they protested but the cost of moving it and having it set up on the land they owned in Snyder County would be too much – too much for them at the time. Again – no problem. He would pay to have the trailer moved from upstate New York to their land in central Pennsylvania and would foot the bill of having the mobile home set up – water, electric, tie-downs - anything they wanted.

Slightly suspicious of such a good deal, for free, no less, the family took a day or so to consider. They checked the place out. It was somewhat modern, maybe from the early seventies or late sixties and it was nice and solid, a far cry better than what they were living in now with their two children. They took the man up on the offer.

A few weeks later the trailer was delivered and set up on their wooded property in Penn's Creek, Pennsylvania. The home had found a home.

The family lived in the trailer for several years with their two children while they were building a house on the same property. Eventually that house was finished and the trailer was left vacant – for a while. Children grow up, get married, have families of their own and it was the same for them. Their youngest daughter, Cristi, married and had two boys. Cristi and her husband were given the trailer as a gift from her parents and it became their home. That is when the sightings began.

Cristi's eldest son refused to walk the hallway to his bedroom at the far end of the trailer at night. Too often he had seen the woman in the long white nightgown carrying the baby. The younger boy, too, had seen the woman in the white nightgown and also required an escort to the bathroom and to bed at night. Cristi had glimpsed the sorry looking spirit mother herself on occasion but was more intrigued by it than frightened. They had all heard the baby cry and had glimpsed the woman pacing back and forth up and down the hall trying to shush the spirit baby as it lay whimpering in her arms.

So, the free trailer had come with strings attached by way of spirits and hauntings. In Cristi's mind it didn't seem to make sense to have dumped such a nice solid home for free just on account of a woman in a nightgown and a crying baby. So what if it was haunted. Other than its sudden appearances on occasion the ghost never bothered them. For Cristi it really had no more impact than the sudden appearance of a mouse darting across a quiet room. It wasn't pleasant to see the ghost, Cristi thought, but it wasn't so unpleasant as to make them move out. That is, until one night when, ironically enough, they were all packed up and ready to move out of the trailer the next day.

Cristi's husband had been accepted at a school in Pittsburgh and they would leave the family homestead for a while as he completed the courses and got his degree. Boxes of personal items had already been loaded into the van. The furniture in the trailer would stay. After all, they would be back in a year. Cristi and her boys sat in the living room watching TV – the last night, for a while at least, in their old home. Cristi lay on the sofa and both boys lounged on the floor in front of the sofa. All of a sudden, the older boy sat bolt upright.

"Look!" he shouted, and pointed in the direction of the TV set directly across the room. Cristi jumped. At first she couldn't understand what had startled her son until the TV that she had been watching slowly faded from view and another scene took its place. Across the room from where she and her boys sat at the sofa, here appeared another sofa, a plaid sofa, colonial style and as Cristi remembers, nicer than the one they had. On the sofa cowered the woman in the long white nightgown. She was crying, her face contorted with fear and pain. The baby's muffled cries could barely be heard, so tightly did she hold it to her breast. This time, however, another spirit had broken the bounds of death, of the past, and appeared to Cristi and her children. A man in dirty, worn, bell-bottom blue jeans, with long stringy hair tied back in a leather thong and several tattoos on his arms appeared in front of the woman and her baby. He angrily paced back and forth screaming obscenities and aiming directly at the baby and the woman at point blank range – a shotgun!

"If we were not all packed up and ready to move out the next day, we would have left anyways," Cristi says now. "I wouldn't have stayed another night in that place – now – knowing what happened in that FREE trailer."

Going on style of clothing and hair, Cristi looked into the background of triple murder suicides that occurred in upstate New York during the early seventies and found nineteen such events on the books. Whether or not these tragedies are still playing themselves out in the spirit world is not known. But the particular tragedy that Cristi and her boys witnessed via the spirit realm doesn't recur in the trailer in Penn's Creek anymore. Within a year the vacated free trailer caught fire and burned to the ground. The woods of Penn's Creek have claimed the charred remains.

The Painter

It is pretty common to call the mountain lion or cougar a panther or "painter" here in central PA. Here's what happened:

In March of the winter of 1994, the winter of the big snows, we had seven feet of snow here in Snyder County and the kids could step over our clothesline. One Saturday morning I heard our dog, Blue, a German Shepherd mix, barking and barking at something down by the creek. He sat on top of the hard pack snow about half way between the house and the creek, which is about a quarter mile away. I walked outside barefoot in the snow, coat over my nightgown to see what was making him bark so. Looking down toward the creek I saw weaving in and about the bare trees two of the biggest cats I had ever seen.

I ran into the house and got the binoculars to get a better look and DID! The cats were tan and they were BIG! Through the binoculars they looked bigger than Blue, an eighty-five pound dog. They had long draping tails that dragged along the top of the snow cover and they slunk along just like big housecats on the prowl. I ran back into the house and yelled for Greg to come have a look. He had been sound asleep and after stumbling outside in his pajamas he fumbled a lot with the binoculars. He said he saw "something," but he didn't see the big cats as plainly as I had seen them.

Now Blue was a smart dog. Although he had snared many a woodchuck and rabbit on occasion and would bark at critters that roamed the property lines if it was bigger than he was, he wouldn't chase it. He sat still as stone while he watched these critters.

I had heard of a guy in Snyder County who had a couple of caged rescue cougars so I called the State Police to ask if they might have escaped. They called him, then called me back and said that his were in their pens.

Several months later we went to a talk at the Snyder County Historical Society where Simon Bonner was giving a talk about Henry Shoemaker. Henry Shoemaker was a folklorist from the turn of the century and had written about panthers in Pennsylvania. Mr. Bonner talked about the panther stories that Shoemaker had written. Thinking that all panthers were black, I asked, "So what color are *these* Pennsylvania 'panthers?'" He said they are actually mountain lions and that they are tan.

A woman came up to me afterwards and asked why I had asked the question and I told her of the sighting earlier that year. She said her husband had seen such creatures up on Shade Mountain when he was hunting but the game commission would not confirm their existence in this area.

We have heard via the underground grapevine of local talk that panthers have been reintroduced to Pennsylvania and allowed to live in this area as a control of the deer population. They are supposed to be shy creatures

74

and not a great threat to humans or livestock. They have the deer.

This is a TRUE STORY!

(I read a story afterwards that it is said that spirit panthers show themselves on occasion. Did Blue bark at a ghost?)

Painting by Sandy Bruce

Big Brown Panther

A song by Greg Burgess

So there, lady, don't think I'm extinct.

Sidehill Phil saw me, so he thinks.

He called the Game Commissioner, but they said "no,

There's no big panthers here that we know."

I'm a big brown panther. (Big brown panther!)

I'm a big brown panther. (Big brown panther!)

I'm a big brown panther,

And I'm still roamin' these hills.

I like rabbits and squirrels and such for lunch,

Or anything from a garbage truck.

I even eat dogs, coyotes, and fishes.

I got long sharp teeth and a tail that swishes.

I'm a big brown panther. (Big brown panther!)

I'm a big brown panther. (Big brown panther!)

I'm a big brown panther,

And I'm still roamin' these hills.

So, little girl, if you're on your own,

Don't think that you're all alone.

You hear a loud holler comin' from the trees,

You'd better run home 'cuz it might be me.

I'm a big brown panther. (Big brown panther!)

I'm a big brown panther. (Big brown panther!)

I'm a big brown panther,

And I'm still roamin' these hills

Owl Medicine

I look to the east and watch the sun rise. I thank God for the day and for the hills, for the corn, for the dried stumps of corn and soybeans, for the pheasants that walk by, for the deer, for the space.

One day I found an owl. It was a very bright Saturday morning. The air was clear, dry, warm. It was late spring. It seemed like I was the only one awake in the world and I was driving, just driving down the road near my home. I was on a highway. It was odd that no one else was awake but it was just as well. I scan the sides of the road when I drive. I'm very careful. You never know when a deer or a child or a dog might run in front of the

78

truck. I take great care not to kill things. I saw the bird lying on the shoulder of the road, gold feathers catching the sunlight, soft wind lifting them from its body. It was dead. Someone else had killed it.

My first thought was greedy. It was like I had seen a pile of gold money lying by the road. I wanted the feathers, not to sell, but to have. I brought the truck to a stop, taking great care to pull far enough off so that a passing motorist would not kill me. I looked all around. It is against the law to pick up a road kill. A game warden had told me that once. It's in our laws.

The owl was fresh killed, fresh dead, its neck was broken. It was still soft and pliable. Someone else must be awake, I thought. I looked up and down the road, off to the hills – then opened up the door to the truck and put the owl on the floor. Poor owl, I thought. Poor, poor owl. I still wanted its feathers.

When I got home I carried the owl to our chicken coop. Our chickens don't like that coop. They moved out long ago and now live in a pen that they chose themselves. I keep dead things in the old chicken coop now, lay deer skulls, tails, and legs on the shelves to dry. That day the coop was empty. I laid the owl on a high shelf, stroked it with my hand and said again, "Poor owl."

When I went into the house my husband was awake and the kitchen smelled of coffee and bacon. The dog was licking out a pan. He stopped for a moment, came over to me and sniffed my boots, my knees, and finally my hand.

"I found an owl," I said to my husband. "You have to see it. It's beautiful! It's dead."

He raised his eyebrows, then sighed, "You can't have it, you know."

"So," I said. "I couldn't leave it by the road to rot." He went outside, peed, then he walked to the coop. When he came back to the house he told me that it was a beautiful owl.

"What are you going to do with it?"

"I don't know. I don't know if they're good luck or bad luck."

We bought our house from Milton, an old man who was murdered one night. Milton had owned an auction house and must have turned a bad deal. That's what everyone said. He owned all the land around our place and leased it to a local farmer for planting corn and soybeans. We had bought a few acres in the midst of all his land. We staked it out. Our patch.

Once a month or so when the moon was dark Milton would burn all the things that had not sold at the auction. Sometimes the pile was amazingly high, like a mountain. Milton would douse it with kerosene and toss a match at the pile. It would blaze up. Then Milton would dance around the fire nervously with a rake as if he could stop the fire from traveling if it wanted to do so. We could watch Milton's silhouette from our porch.

"God! What is he -- nuts?" we would remark to each other. "He looks like the devil." And we would laugh.

My son had a dream the day before Milton got killed. He came downstairs in the morning and asked me quick for something to eat. I handed him some bread. It's bad luck to tell a dream before breakfast so we always eat something first, then tell.

"I dreamed about a pumpkin," he said. "But I didn't like it."

"What about the pumpkin?"

"The mouth was filled with candy but the candy was spilling out – it was all over the place. It was ugly."

I thought about this dream and found it ugly as well. Normally I would have told my son what his dream meant but the feeling it gave me was not good. "It means you shouldn't eat too much candy," I lied. That night Milton got his throat slit. It made us wary of strangers.

Milton's kids didn't want to be farmers and they didn't want to keep the land in the family. There were too many of them. They decided to sell it all to the highest bidder and split up the money.

Milton had once lived in the old house that sold with the land. He had lived there with his seven kids and his wife Ellen. She died of cancer. When she died he closed off the bedroom, scattered the kids to the hills and moved out. He locked the door to her room, stuffed the keyhole with paper, then rented the place out to poor folk who couldn't afford better. He said they could have run of the house – except the room that was locked. He said he kept stuff in there.

We got to know the family that moved into the house. They said that they poked the tissue out of the lock of the forbidden room and peeked inside. They said that pill bottles still crowded the nightstand, that the bedcovers had never been drawn back over the white sheets, that a wooden chair was placed close to the bed and still faced the pillows. They said that they could still see the depression in the mattress where Milton's wife had died. It was like death had suddenly snatched the whole family away when it arrived to claim Ellen.

It gave them the creeps. They ran by the door at night when they went to bed. When Milton got murdered his eldest son told the family that they would have to move out of the house. They told me that they didn't mind. They didn't want to stay there anymore anyway – too creepy, they said. Maybe Milton would come back to sit in the chair in the locked room, throat slit, eyes open, staring at the sheets.

On the morning of the auction the people gathered like birds, vultures, shoulders squared, hands deep in their pockets, nervously looking here and there as if for spilled corn or carrion. One by one as they lost out, they stepped back, speaking in hushed tones as the bidding went higher and higher. The land didn't sell to a farmer as all who live in this valley had hoped. It sold to a developer who would eat the land itself, leave it littered with houses like droppings, then move on to eat more land.

The man who had worked Milton's land all those years shook his head as he walked to his truck, a hollow

smile on his face. After a short time Milton's house was knocked down and carried off. Anything left was piled high and burned.

When winter came the snow was higher than we had ever seen it. It was very cold, so cold that the trees in the hills sounded like shotguns as their branches swelled with the cold and exploded. The chickens stayed in their pen, combs and waddles black and frostbitten, and each morning I would tread over many feet of hard-pack snow path to give them food and water. The owl lay asleep, silently drying in the old coop. I maintained a suspicion of strangers who occasionally came up the lane to our house. I became suspicious of friends.

I listened as ice fell from the sky, listened as trees succumbed to its weight and fell over in the woods. The fields lay like a broad sea around us, smooth waves of solid white, even the dried stalks of corn from the autumn harvest were covered up. When it didn't snow and the sun came out we were blinded by a world white and glaring. When we went into the house we were still blind.

One morning I woke to the sound of the dog barking. Barking. Barking. Barking. It was an alarm. He wanted me to see something. When I stepped onto the porch, a blanket over my shoulders, boots over bare feet, I saw him sitting on top of the frozen snow and looking down toward the creek.

"What do you see, boy?" I asked him. I looked toward the creek and saw two great cats strolling through the bare saplings. They moved like snakes and glided in and out, in and out, one following the other. They were tan and had long draping tails that brushed the snow as they walked. We watched them until they were out of sight, then I went in and woke my husband.

"I just saw something," I told him.

"What? What did you see?" He was still half asleep.

"I saw some big cats – bigger than any I've ever

seen." I told him what they looked like and he said cats like that didn't live around here anymore.

"Maybe they're hungry," I said. "Maybe they live up in the mountains far away, but are coming to the farms to find food." He got up, put on his robe and went outside to look. They were gone.

"I don't see anything," he said.

A few days later I tried to walk across the field to the creek, look for tracks, and almost became overcome with the weariness of walking through the snow. The air had warmed some, and soft pockets grabbed my legs and pulled them under, making it almost impossible to walk. I felt as if I was dying. If the big cats had left tracks they would have to remain unseen, I thought, and be covered by more snow, then erased by the sun. It was too dangerous to go looking for them. After that I just studied the creek from the safety of the house but never saw the big cats again – just gray trees and snow.

Once when I was younger and very troubled I tried to drive to the Yukon. A man I thought I loved had lied to me and had disappeared one day. He had told me he was going out for a minute and then he never came back. I thought that if I could drive to the Yukon and would see nothing but white, I would have an uninterrupted view so that I could not think. I wanted to set a wooden chair in the midst of a snowfield and just sit there, the entire world white around me as though it had disappeared. I didn't make it that far because on the way there I met a woman who seemed to have more troubles than I did. Her man beat her. She was drunk and I kept watch over her as she dragged me from bar to bar and got drunker. She asked me to drive her home and have something to eat. She wanted me to meet her husband. She said her husband wouldn't beat her in front of anyone; in fact he'd probably be really friendly. After a while I had to leave and she looked nervous, bit her lip. The Yukon seemed too far away by then and I was tired, so I went home. As the years passed I became able to accept disappointments and the desire to see nothing became frightening.

I look to the west and thank God for a day that has passed, for long shadows, for the nervous talk of the birds before they go to roost, the flutter of the moth and hungry bats, for the silent sweep and breath of an owl's wings as it closes in on a mouse.

One evening in late winter Homer came by to visit. The dog had barked as he pulled into the driveway and we stepped outside to see who had come.

"Hey, Homer," I said as he worked his way around the snow piles. He was always very careful about the steps he took. Homer is an old man and knows a lot. Sometimes he talks so much that I think I won't possibly remember all that he says and I don't. He has lived in the valley all his life and knows stories about the people and families that have lived here. A woman was with him. She was dark, all dressed in black leather with fringe and wore long earrings. She looked tough, like a biker. She said she was an Indian.

"What brings you here, Homer?"

"Ah, maybe just a little cabin fever," he said. "I was on my way to the store and thought I'd pay a visit." He introduced his friend, said she was driving. I made coffee and we sat around the kitchen table, talking and smoking and telling stories. I told them about the big cats I had seen. My husband sighed and said that he didn't see them.

"She thinks they're hungry," he said.

Homer seemed surprised that I had seen such animals and said that panthers used to live in these hills but that as far as he knew the last one had been killed a long time ago. He said that sometimes panthers came back as ghosts.

"Well, the dog saw them, too," I said.

I asked him about owls. The woman who had come with him got very excited when I mentioned owls and said she knew all about them, had read a book about owl medicine. She said that when an owl floated by a person on silent wings it was good. It gave the person wisdom and eyes that could see through darkness and inside people. An owl that came as a result of a violent death brought sadness. Its feathers would bring sadness. Homer told a story about a man who had killed owls so that he could sell their feathers to people who wished to be like the Indians. The man had sold motorcycles in the front of his shop – and feathers and bones from the back. He said that the state had closed the place down and that the man was in jail now. My husband looked at me for a moment and Homer and the woman looked at us – one face to the next. I didn't say that I had found an owl and that it was in the coop drying.

They asked about the land around us and said that it was a shame that it was going to have houses put up on it. It was good farmland. Homer said that the whole thing with Milton was a bad deal, but that everyone knew Milton did things that were not quite right. He said Milton always kept one hand behind his back when he cut a deal. The woman dug into her purse and gave me a bag of sage.

"Here," she said. "You can have this. It's nice to burn. You use it to clean stuff – the smoke – use the smoke to clean stuff."

After they left I wished that I could get rid of the owl, bury it, but the ground was still frozen and the snow too deep. It would have to wait.

In the spring the snow melted slowly, slowly enough that the water didn't carry the land with it as it streamed down the ridge. The spring freshets ran as usual as though nothing had happened, as though the winter had not been long. The chickens came out of their pen and poked at the mud for worms, insects, swollen corn that had been dropped as I carried it to them throughout the winter. The owl was quite dry now, the feathers light and loose. Those that had drifted to the floor of the coop I picked up and placed back on the shelf, tucking them carefully beneath its body. I had long since lost the desire to keep any of its feathers.

I look to the south and thank God for the sun, for the

heat of the day, for sweat, for birds that come back and for
wind, thunder, and rain that falls in torrents, washes
everything clean, then sinks deep into the earth so that I
can draw it out and drink it.

Sometime near the end of spring, a full year, I decided that it was time to bury the owl that I had found that had lain dead in the coop for so long. I didn't tell anybody that I was going to bury it. Who would care? When it comes time to bury things that have died there should be a ceremony, something that makes the passage certain. I was afraid to bury this owl, I feared for its sad medicine, feared touching it anymore. Poor owl, I thought. Poor, poor owl. It couldn't help the way it died – the unseeing eyes of a passing motorist, the negligence of itself.

Early in the morning just after sunrise I dressed and gathered up a few items of ceremony – a stone, some of the sage, a piece of cardboard on which to carry the owl, some matches. Then I carried it to the creek along with a shovel. The morning was already warm. Late spring, the sun was higher.

I crossed the creek because burying it on the other side seemed more right than to bury it on our home side. I dug a hole, placed the owl in it, covered it, placed the stone on the mark, and then put some of the sage on the stone. My thoughts were quiet, only on the task at hand, no prayers, no special words. The match lit easily. As the flame touched the sage it immediately began to burn, then smolder to a thick white smoke. I could hear geese on their

way north, flying from the southern sky. As the smoke
from the sage billowed more and more, a breeze caught
hold of it and carried it east. The day.

The same breeze caught the smoke again and carried
it to the west. The lengthening shadows. It touched it

again and pushed it toward the south. The birds that come back. The air became very still and the smoke rose straight up for a moment. The geese that had been distant came to fly right overhead. I looked up and saw them part ranks as though allowing another bird to enter their formation to fly with them. The wind stirred again. It took hold of the smoke this time pulling it to the north.

I look to the north and thank God for things that come and go, for sleep and for the pure white space that asks nothing, says nothing, shows nothing.

About the Authors

Beverley Conrad will pretty much believe anything anyone tells her especially if they start out with, "Hey, do you want to hear a story? It's true." She will in turn pass the story on as it was told to her, slathering a little extra jam on the bread where necessary as a way of filling in details.

A musician, artist and writer for many years, she is a twice published author and has a great deal of writing on the Internet about music and food. Known locally as the Fiddlerwoman, she often combines stories and music into historical and imaginative presentations. She and Greg met at Grand Central Station in NYC thirty something years ago. For more stories and writing about the fiddle, visit her website at www.fiddlerwoman.com. She lives outside of Selinsgrove, PA, in a haunted house in Salem Swamp.

Gregory Burgess, best known for his skills as a musician, has published fiction, poetry, and nonfiction in *The Journal of Experimental Fiction, neotrope, gestalten, The Seed, Indian-Artifacts Magazine,* and *Paranormal Pennsylvania,* as well as online. He lives with his wife, Beverley, and the ghost of George Row in an old farmhouse in the Bloody Triangle, surrounded nightly by prowling brown panthers and headless dogs.